The Story Girl

Book 7

™

Dedicated to my six grandchildren, the "cousins," especially to Bethany, for whom I began this journey with the "Story Girl" on "The Golden Road," six years ago. I pray all of you will find these stories about the King cousins a wonderful example for you to follow in holiness, purity, and real fun—and help you along your own journey to the heart of God.

From the author of Anne of Green Gables

L.M. Montgomery

The Story Girl
Book 7

™

MIDNIGHT MADNESS AND MAYHEM

Adapted by Barbara Davoll

zonder**kidz**

zonderkidz.
The children's group of Zondervan

www.zonderkidz.com

Midnight Madness and Mayhem
Copyright © 2005 The Zondervan Corporation, David Macdonald, trustee
and Ruth Macdonald

Requests for information should be addressed to:
Grand Rapids, Michigan 49530

Library of Congress Cataloging-in-Publication Data

Davoll, Barbara.
   Midnight madness and mayhem / by Barbara Davoll ; adapted from The
story girl by L.M. Montgomery.
      p. cm.–(The story girl ; bk. 7)
   Summary: On Prince Edward Island during a summer in the nineteenth
century, the King cousins participate in a school concert which has a
surprising conclusion for the Story Girl, finally see the contents of the blue
trunk, and learn a startling secret.
   ISBN 10: 0–310–70861–3 (softcover; ISBN 13: 978–0310–70861–2
   [1. Storytellers—Fiction. 2. Cousins—Fiction. 3. Conduct of life—Fiction.
4. Prince Edward Island—History—19th century—Fiction.
5. Canada—History—19th century—Fiction.] I. Montgomery, L. M. (Lucy
Maud), 1874-1942. Story girl. II. Title.
   PZ7.D3216Mi 2006
   [Fic]–dc22   2004012270

Editor: Amy DeVries
Interior design: Susan Ambs
Art direction: Merit Alderink
Cover illustrations: Jim Griffin

Printed in the United States of America

05 06 07 /OPM/ 10 9 8 7 6 5 4 3 2 1

Contents

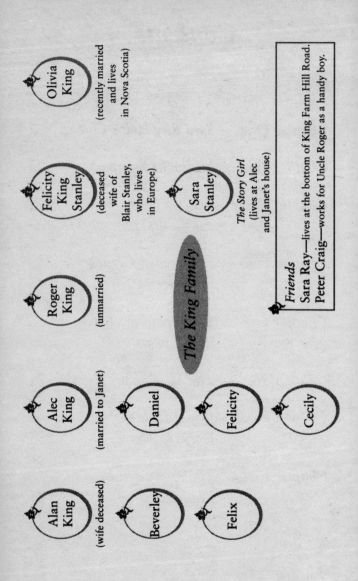

The King Family

Alan King (wife deceased)

Alec King (married to Janet)

Roger King (unmarried)

Felicity King Stanley (deceased wife of Blair Stanley, who lives in Europe)

Olivia King (recently married and lives in Nova Scotia)

Beverley

Felix

Daniel

Felicity

Cecily

Sara Stanley
The Story Girl (lives at Alec and Janet's house)

Friends
Sara Ray—lives at the bottom of King Farm Hill Road.
Peter Craig—works for Uncle Roger as a handy boy.

Sara Ray Helps Out

Felicity came flying down the stairs
and called her mother. Aunt Janet
went upstairs and quickly came back
down with a grim look on her face. A few
minutes later she hustled back upstairs
with a large pan of warm water.

Chapter One

Aunt Olivia was married. We could hardly believe it. What a hole was left in the King family. The wedding had been such a highlight in our lives, and now it was hard for us to get back to normal. We kept wondering how our favorite aunt liked her new home in Halifax, Nova Scotia. It seemed she was a whole world away from the King farm on Prince Edward Island. Did she miss us as much as we missed her?

I might as well tell you right off that my name is Beverley King, and I am the oldest of the King cousins. I've always thought that my mother chose the name Beverley because she wanted a girl and was surprised to learn that she had gotten a boy instead. My friends all call me Bev, and I hope you will too.

Just so you can keep us all straight, Uncle Alec and Aunt Janet are the parents of Dan, Felicity, and Cecily. They are kind, loving parents and agreed that my brother, Felix, and I could stay with them for a year while my father opened his new business office in South America. Our mother died when we were very small, and it seemed good to have Aunt Janet mother us and give us good-night kisses.

It is clear that Aunt Janet misses Aunt Olivia as much as we do. Aunt Olivia, who had been a housekeeper for her brother, our uncle Roger, spent a good bit of time running between their farm and ours. She and Aunt Janet shared recipes and tasty tidbits of gossip. Now poor Aunt Janet had to keep herself busy, and I could tell she was lonely without her friend.

The Story Girl, our cousin Sara Stanley, had lived next door with Aunt Olivia until the wedding. When Aunt Olivia left the island, Sara came to live with all of us at Uncle Alec's house on the King farm. That meant some adjustments of course.

A strong competition exists between Felicity and Sara Stanley. Sara is fourteen, a year older than Felicity and a favorite with all of us. She is such fun and a gifted storyteller. She often keeps us spellbound with her wonderful tales. I think Felicity is jealous of her, although she herself is quite beautiful and a fantastic cook for thirteen years of age. Just the same, she knows she isn't adored like the Story Girl.

In just a few weeks it felt like the Story Girl, Sara Stanley, had always lived on the King farm. Anyway, life returned to normal at Uncle Alec's, broken by ripples of excitement and letters from Aunt Olivia describing her honeymoon trip. All of us cousins were writing and printing a newspaper we called *Our Magazine.* So we decided to print her letters in our newspaper under the heading "From a Special Correspondent." We were very proud of the column, in which our town had shown a lot of interest.

The school concert, always held in June, was an exciting event in our young lives. It was the first time any of us had been on a platform, and some of us were very nervous. We all had recitations except Dan, who flatly refused to take part.

"No way will you get me up on that stage where everybody on earth can make fun of me," he stated.

"I hardly think 'everybody on earth' will be at our little school program," the Story Girl said, poking fun at Dan.

"Well, it's everybody on earth that I know," argued Dan, "and I ain't doing it."

"I know I'll just die when I get up on that platform facing people," sighed Sara Ray, as we talked over the affair the night before the concert.

Sara Ray is not our cousin, but she is a special friend of Cecily and lives at the foot of the hill, just below the King farm. She is all right as a friend, I guess, but she does a lot of complaining and whining. We always include her in our fun, though, since she and Cecily are such good friends.

"I'm not one single bit nervous," said Felicity with a yawn.

"I'm not nervous this time," said the Story Girl, "but the first time I recited I was."

"I'm afraid I'll faint," remarked Cecily.

"My aunt Jane said that when you have to speak in public, you should pretend you're just speaking to a bunch of cabbage heads," said Peter.

Peter Craig isn't our cousin either. He has been working as Uncle Roger's handy boy. But recently his father, who had been a hopeless drunk, was converted. Now that Peter's father is a Christian, he is taking care of his family. Peter is just finishing out his contract for the year with Uncle Roger, and then he won't have to work anymore. We are all very glad, because Peter is a smart young man, and now he will be able to go to school more.

"I don't know much about the cabbage heads, Peter," said the Story Girl. "I want to recite to *people* and see them looking interested and thrilled. I've never seen a cabbage head look interested in anything."

"If I can only get through what I have to say at the program without crying, I don't care if I thrill people or not," said Sara Ray.

"I'm afraid I'll forget my piece and get stuck," worried Felix. "Some of you be sure and prompt me if I do. And do it quick, so I won't get rattled worse."

"I know one thing," said Cecily resolutely, "and that is, I'm going to curl my hair for tomorrow night. I've never curled it since that night Peter almost died. But I really must for tomorrow night. All the other girls are going to have theirs in curls."

"The dew and heat will take all of the curl out, and you'll look like a scarecrow," warned Felicity.

"No, I won't. I'm going to put my hair up in papers tonight and wet it with curling fluid that Judy Pineau, the Ray's hired girl, uses. Sara Ray loaned me a bottle of it. Judy says it is great stuff. Your hair will stay curled for days, no matter how damp the weather. I'll leave the papers in my hair until tomorrow, and then I'll have beautiful curls for the concert."

"You'd better leave your hair alone," said Dan gruffly. "Smooth hair is better than a lot of flyaway curls."

But Cecily was not to be persuaded. Curls she craved and curls she meant to have.

"I'm thankful my welts and wasp stings have all gone away," said Sara Ray.

That night Cecily put her hair up in curl papers, after soaking them thoroughly in Judy Pineau's curling fluid. It was a nasty job, but she got it done. Then she went to sleep with a towel tied over her head to protect the pillow. She slept well, dreaming of the lovely curls soon to come. When she came down to breakfast the next morning, the Story Girl told her she thought she ought to take her curls down right away.

"Oh, no," Cecily answered. "If I do, my hair will be straight again by night. I'm going to leave them on until the last minute."

"I wouldn't do that—I really wouldn't," objected the Story Girl. "If you do your hair will be too curly and all bushy and fuzzy."

Finally Cecily decided that she would heed the advice and take her hair down. She and the two older girls disappeared up the stairs, and the next thing we heard was a little shriek—then two or three more. Felicity came flying down the stairs and called her mother. Aunt Janet went upstairs and quickly came back down with a grim look on her face. A few minutes later she hustled back upstairs with a large pan of warm water.

When Felicity came downstairs, we bombarded her with questions.

"What on earth is the matter with Cecily?" demanded Dan. "Is she sick?"

"Well, no . . . she isn't sick," Felicity answered. "I warned her not to put her hair in curls, but she wouldn't listen to me. I guess she wishes she had now. When people don't have naturally curly hair they shouldn't try to make it curly."

"Never mind all that, Felicity," interrupted her brother, Dan. "Just tell me what's wrong with Sis."

"Well . . . it seems that ninny, Sara Ray, mistook a bottle of glue for Judy's curling fluid. Cecily put

14

her hair up with *that*," Felicity confided. "It's an awful sight!"

"Oh, my word," said Dan. We all thought of Cecily as our favorite, and we hated to see her in such a mess. "Will she ever get it out?"

"Who knows? She's soaking her head in a dishpan. Her hair is just matted together hard as a board. That's what comes of vanity," said Felicity in her holier-than-thou way. No girl with more vanity ever lived than smarty-mouth Felicity.

Poor Cecily had paid dearly enough for *her* vanity. She spent most of the morning soaking her head in warm water with her eyes closed. Finally her hair was soft enough to untangle it from the curl papers. She looked like a plucked chicken with the little white papers stuck all over her head.

Aunt Janet gave Cecily the shampoo of her lifetime, trying to remove the sticky glue from her long curls. We could hear her crying all the way downstairs. Time was getting short, and soon we would have to leave for the school concert. In those days there were no hair dryers, so Cecily had to sit in front of the hot oven with her hair hanging in her face. Finally it was dry. But it was dull and dry, not smooth and lovely as usual.

"I am such a mess," she moaned, looking in the mirror at herself. "Just look how the ends stick out. It looks like dried hay!"

"Sara Ray is a perfect idiot," stormed Dan. "It's all right, Sis. I don't think it's too bad," he soothed.

"Oh, don't be so hard on poor Sara," said Cecily. "She didn't mean to bring me glue. It's really my own fault. I made a solemn vow when Peter was dying I would never curl my hair again. I should have kept it. It isn't right to break solemn vows. But my hair will look like hay tonight."

Poor Sara Ray felt terrible when she came up and found out that she had given Cecily the wrong stuff. Felicity was very hard on Sara and told her she didn't have sense enough to come in out of the rain. "Imagine! Giving my sister glue!" she railed. Even Aunt Janet was not her usual warm self, but was cold and disapproving to Sara Ray.

But sweet Cecily forgave her totally, and they walked to the school that night with their arms around each other. Cecily was a loyal friend to Sara Ray even when all the rest of us lost patience with her.

The schoolroom was crowded with friends and neighbors. Mr. Perkins, the schoolteacher, was flying about getting things ready. Miss Reade, who was going to play the organ for us, was already in her place looking sweet and pretty. She wore a white lace hat, with a little bunch of forget-me-not flowers around the brim. Her dress was a white muslin with a blue violet pattern.

"Doesn't she look angelic?" said Sara Ray with a sigh. She and Cecily adored Miss Reade and had all sorts of notions about her. "Look! There is the 'Awkward Man.' I bet he came to hear her play. He's never come to a concert at school before."

"He may have come to hear the Story Girl recite," said Felicity. "He is a good friend of hers too."

All of this conversation was about a tall, lanky neighbor of ours who was called the "Awkward Man." We called him that because he was always tripping or in some way being awkward, especially when girls were around. The girls had cooked up some notion that the lovely Miss Reade might be in love with the Awkward Man. I felt this was not likely.

The concert was successful. Each of us said our "pieces" well. Felix got through his recitations without getting "stuck" as he thought he might. Peter did a great job, even though he stuffed his hands in his pockets the entire time. Mr. Perkins had been trying to break him of that habit, along with not pausing for commas.

When Peter rehearsed his recitation, the teacher would coach him, saying, "Stop, stop, Peter. There's a semicolon in that line. Don't murder it, please."

That night Peter did remember not to murder his semicolon, and Cecily didn't faint or fail when it came her turn. She did a lovely job. In fact, I thought she might have done it even better than ever, knowing that her hair didn't look just right and wanting to make up for it some way.

As she was going up to recite, I heard a woman behind me say that Cecily King didn't look well. She said she was "thin and sickly looking, just like her aunt who had died from pneumonia when she was young."

That comment made me so mad I could hardly stand it. I wanted to tell the woman to be quiet and mind her own business. All of us were concerned about the dry, hacking cough that had bothered Cecily all year. And there were other symptoms that seemed to worry Uncle Alec and Aunt Janet. Cecily was such a dear little cousin to me. I had a red face for the rest of the evening, remembering the woman's words.

Even Sara Ray did well, although she couldn't disguise her nervousness. Dan said, "When she bowed at the end, she looked like her head worked on a wire." We were all relieved when she stepped off the stage. Sara was, in a sense, one of our crowd, and we had been afraid she would disgrace us by doing poorly or crying.

Of all the cousins, Felicity did the poorest. Although beautiful, she had no imagination and recited her part without enthusiasm or expression. But what did it matter? To look at her, with her brilliant blue eyes, golden curls, and lovely face, was enough. I'm sure everyone felt it was worth the ten cents they paid just to look at her. Nobody can have everything.

The Story Girl followed Felicity. When she stood to recite, it seemed as if everyone was breathless. Mr. Perkins' face lost the look of tense anxiety he had worn all evening. Here was a performer he could depend on. No need to fear that she would falter because of stage fright or forgetfulness. Her piece was an old one that we'd all heard many times, but when she began, the magic of her voice caught and held her listeners spellbound.

All of us knew her recitation by heart, as it was included in one of our school readers—a poem about an old lady who had been married to a cold and cruel husband. As the story goes, the woman died and was buried in a rich, beautiful tomb provided by her family.

But sadly, the woman had not died at all, but was unconscious. In the middle of the night, she awoke and escaped from her tomb. Chilled and terrified, she made her way to her husband's door. He, thinking she was a ghost, drove her away into the night. Then she went to her father's home and received no welcome there. In a pitiful condition, she wandered the dark, lonely streets until she fell at the door of her former suitor.

He was unafraid and took her in. The next day her husband and father discovered her empty tomb and came to claim her. She refused to return to them, and the case was carried to the court of law. The court judged that since she had been pronounced dead, she was no longer a daughter or wife and had no legal ties to her family.

The Story Girl recited the poem with great expression, pausing where needed for emphasis and dramatic intensity. She had often recited it for us, and we hung on her every word. In the court scene, as she recited, she became the stern judge, the pitiful woman who was wronged, the unfair father, and the cruel husband.

As she built the recitation, using the loudness and softness of her voice for expression, she came to the climax of the entire poem.

"The court pronounces the defendant—"

The Story Girl paused for a breathless moment to bring out the tragic importance of the last word.

"*Dead,*" piped up Sara Ray in her shrill, whiny voice.

The effect of Sara Ray taking away the climax of the Story Girl's recitation can only be imagined. Instead of the sigh of relieved tension that should have swept over the audience at the concluding line, there was a great burst of laughter. The Story Girl's performance was completely spoiled.

She gave Sara Ray a version of a "look that could kill," stumbled awkwardly through the concluding lines, and sat down humiliated. Her cheeks were red as fire, and she got up and ran backstage, embarrassed beyond words. Mr. Perkins was furious, and the audience kept giggling and laughing for the rest of the evening.

Sara Ray had no idea what had happened, and she kept looking around, smiling as the audience laughed. She wanted to be part of the fun. As soon as the concert was over, we surrounded her with a whirlwind of rebukes.

"You little fool," cried Felicity angrily. Although Felicity was jealous of the Story Girl, she couldn't stand having one of our family made to look ridiculous. "You have less sense than anyone I know, Sara Ray."

Poor Sara dissolved in tears. "I didn't know. I thought she was stuck and needed someone to help her out," she wailed.

Sara Ray cried all the way home, but we didn't try to comfort her. We were all too angry. Even her friend Cecily was seriously annoyed. First the glue, and now this. We saw Sara Ray sobbing as she turned into her lane. Although she looked pitiful, none of us cared—at least, not then.

The Story Girl arrived at home before us. We tried to sympathize, but she refused to be comforted.

"Please don't ever mention it to me again," she said with tight lips. "Oh, that little idiot!"

"She spoiled Peter's sermon last summer, and now she's spoiled your recitation," said Felicity with disgust. "Remember how she got so scared when Peter was preaching on hell that she went into hysterics? I think we should quit associating with her."

"Oh, don't be so hard on her," pleaded Cecily. "Think of the hard life she has at home. Her mother is so rough with her. I know she'll cry all night."

"Oh, let's go to bed," growled Dan. "I'm good and ready for it. I've had enough of school concerts." We all agreed as we trudged wearily up the stairs to bed.

Midnight Escapade

Neither of us will ever forget the sweet delight of that stolen walk in the dark. A spell of glamour was over us. The breezes whispered lovely scents of the Junebells growing in the meadow, and the pine trees near our old church bowed to us as we passed by.

Chapter Two

The adventures of that night, with all the excitement and frustration, were over for all but two of us. Silence had settled down over the old house—the eerie, whispered, creeping silence of night. Felix and Dan were already sound asleep, and I was drifting near the shore of dreamland when a light tap on the door awakened me.

"Bev, are you asleep?" came a whisper through the door.

I recognized right away that it was the Story Girl.

"No, what is it?" I whispered back.

"S-s-h-h! Get up, get dressed, and come out. I need you," came her answer.

Struck with concern and curiosity, I obeyed. *What now?* I wondered as I climbed out of my cozy bed.

Outside in the hall I found the Story Girl dressed in her hat and vest.

"Where are you going?" I whispered in amazement.

"Hush. Please say you'll come with me. I've got to go to the school. The clasp on my pearl necklace came loose at the concert. I was so afraid I'd lose it that I took it off and put it up on the bookcase. After the concert, I was so upset that I forgot all about it."

The pearl necklace was a very beautiful one that had belonged to the Story Girl's mother. Only by coaxing Aunt Janet had she been allowed to wear it that night for the first time.

"There's no sense in going for it in the dead of night," I objected. "It will be quite safe. You can go for it in the morning."

"Lizzie Paxton and her daughter are going to clean the school tomorrow," she responded. "I heard Lizzie say tonight that they mean to start cleaning tomorrow morning by five o'clock, before the heat of the day. *You* know what Lizzie's reputation is. If she finds that necklace, I'll never see it again.

"Besides, if I wait till morning, Aunt Janet may find out that I left it there, and she'd never let me wear it again. No, I must go for it now. Of course, if you're afraid . . . ," she added with scorn.

"Afraid? Are you kidding?" I puffed. "Come on, let's go."

We slipped outside without making a sound and found ourselves in the strangeness of a dark night. We had never been out at such an hour, and our hearts tingled with the charm of it. The world seemed an alien place full of enchantment and magic.

Only in the country can one become truly acquainted with the night. The dim, wide fields lie in silence, wrapped in the holy mystery of darkness. The air in the pastures is sweet with the hush of dreams.

"Isn't it wonderful?" breathed the Story Girl as we went down the long King Farm Hill Road. "You know, I can forgive Sara Ray now. Earlier tonight I thought I never could, but now it doesn't seem to matter anymore. I can even see how funny it was. Oh, wasn't it a scream? *'Dead'* in that squeaky little voice of Sara's! Tomorrow I'll just act as if nothing happened. Here in the night, it seems as if it happened long ago."

Neither of us will ever forget the sweet delight of that stolen walk in the dark. A spell of glamour was over us. The breezes whispered lovely scents of the Junebells growing in the meadow, and the pine trees near our old church bowed to us as we passed by.

Fireflies were out in abundance that night. There is certainly something a little supernatural about fireflies. Nobody pretends to understand them, as they flit around like tiny fairies carrying goblin lanterns.

"Isn't it beautiful?" said the Story Girl in awe. "I wouldn't have missed this for anything in the world. I'm glad I left my necklace. And I'm glad you are with me, Bev. The others wouldn't understand so well. I like you because I don't have to talk to you all the time. It's so nice to walk with someone you don't have to talk to.

"Oh, we're coming near the graveyard," Sara whispered as the fence near the old church came into view. "Are you frightened to pass it, Bev?"

"No, I'm not frightened," I answered slowly. "But I have a weird feeling."

"So have I," she said. "But it isn't fear. I don't know what it is. I feel as if ... oh, let's just hurry! Isn't it strange to think of all the dead people in there who were once alive like you and me? I don't feel as if I could *ever* die. Do you?"

"No, but everyone must. Of course, life must go on just the same. Don't let's talk of such things here," I said hurriedly.

I walked up closer to the fence of the cemetery and looked at the markers standing as sentinels over the graves.

"It's important to think about death and the life thereafter, I think," said the Story Girl, still standing in the road. "I'm glad we still have time to learn more about it. Come on, let's hurry. I'm getting chilly now."

When we reached the school, we found a window that had been left open a crack and scrambled in. After lighting a lamp, we found the missing necklace. The Story Girl stood on the platform and gave a funny repeat of her recitation with Sara Ray's interruption.

It made me shout with laughter. We prowled around with delight over being there at an unearthly hour when everybody supposed we were sound asleep in our beds.

It was with regret that we left and walked home as slowly as we could to prolong our midnight adventure.

"Let's never tell anyone," said the Story Girl, as we reached home. "Let's just have it as a secret between us forever—something that nobody else knows a thing about except you and me."

"We'd better keep it a secret from Aunt Janet anyhow," I whispered, laughing. "She'd think we're both crazy."

"It's fun to be crazy once in a while," the Story Girl said.

The soft light of morning was just creeping over the meadow as we came quietly in the door. We would never forget our midnight adventure and the fun of being out on the prowl all night long. It was a secret that belonged just to Sara Stanley and me, and we never told anyone about it.

The next morning we had a special breakfast because it was Felicity's birthday. Since it was Saturday, Aunt Janet had invited our friends—Sara Ray and Peter—to eat with us. Usually Felicity helped Aunt Janet with baking special goodies for our birthdays. But this morning Sara Stanley, our Story Girl, had on a big apron and was bustling around the kitchen helping our aunt prepare blueberry pancakes with yummy maple syrup and big slabs of ham. And, of course, a delicious chocolate birthday cake with Felicity's name on it.

After breakfast Felicity opened her presents. Each of us had made something special for our pretty cousin. There was a stack of birthday cards on the table, and each one was opened and read out loud. Some were funny, given by the boys, and the ones given by the girl cousins and Sara Ray were frilly and pretty.

Underneath all of the cards was a special one made of shiny gold paper and tied together with a blue ribbon.

"Here's another one, Felicity," said Cecily, handing it to her. I knew who it was from, but none of the others knew. I looked at Peter and winked knowingly. We had kept the secret that he was writing a poem—an "ode," as he called it. Felicity's face showed surprise as she opened it and saw that it was simply signed "A Friend." I honestly don't think she had a clue that it was from Peter. She began reading it, and her pretty face turned a rosy pink with pleasure and a little embarrassment. It read:

To Felicity on Her Birthday

O maiden fair with golden hair
And brow of purest white,
I'd fight for you, I'd die for you
Let me be your faithful knight.
This is your birthday, blessed day
You are thirteen years old today
May you be happy and fair as you are now
Until your hair is gray.
I gaze into your shining eyes
They are so blue and bright.
I'd fight for you, I'd die for you
Let me be your faithful knight.

"Not bad, Peter," Felix said leaning across the table.

"Yes, that's very nice, Peter," said Sara Ray. "I never had a poem written about me," she said with a longing.

"It's not a poem; it's an ode," Peter explained.

"What's an ode?" asked Dan. "Sounds like a poem to me."

"I'm afraid *you* couldn't understand," snipped Felicity in her usual nasty way to her brother.

"You might be surprised what I understand, *darling*," responded Dan sarcastically.

Sara Stanley, carrying in the lighted birthday cake, saved us another brother-sister quarrel.

"I know what an ode is, and that one was very nice," the Story Girl affirmed to Peter, as she put the cake on the table in front of Felicity.

"I think it was lovely too," said Felicity quietly with a pretty blush.

That was all the praise Peter needed. As we sang "Happy Birthday," his voice was the loudest and his smile the widest.

A Letter from Aunt Olivia

Suddenly Sara jumped up, and with a muffled "Excuse me," raced up the stairs. She didn't cry often, but we knew the letter was just a bit too much.

Chapter Three

One afternoon Dan came home from the post office with a large fat envelope from Aunt Olivia. Aunt Janet insisted we wait until after supper to read it so that Uncle Alec, Uncle Roger, and Peter could hear it too. After supper the girls quickly finished the dish washing, and we gathered around the table to listen as Aunt Janet read:

> My Dearest Family,
> and Especially My Sweet
> Nephews and Nieces,
>
> My life has been such a whirlwind since our arrival here in Nova Scotia that I haven't been able to manage anything like a real letter. But now I'm able to squeeze out a bit of time and write to you, my dear loved ones. I will begin with the beginning.
>
> Our honeymoon, as you know, was wonderful, but the ferry crossing to Nova Scotia was a bit rough as the winds were high that day. Many aboard the ship were quite seasick, and as soon as

it was realized that Robert was a doctor, he was pressed into service. I fared quite well and was just a bit squeamish when we were in the roughest waters. But I was able to care for a little baby whose mother was quite seasick.

Upon arrival in Halifax, we went immediately to our new home, which is situated on a high cliff overlooking the ocean, probably one of the prettiest locations in all of Halifax. I can't wait to welcome each of you here, perhaps even next year. We have plenty of room so that you may all have a room of your own. I really am surprised at the excellent taste that Robert has, and "The Cliffs," as we call our home, is beautiful.

As soon as Robert discovered that I play the piano, he ordered a large grand piano, which was delivered before we arrived. I do love it and play it a lot. In fact, I even have some piano students.

At the mention of the piano, Felicity rolled her eyes at the Story Girl. All the girl cousins would love to have a piano to play. When Aunt Janet read that each of us could have our own room, Felix leaned over to me and said, "Uncle Robert must be rich!" I agreed. Aunt Janet continued reading:

I can't describe the joy that I find in being Robert's wife and taking care of our home. I have to admit to some homesickness, however, and wonder how Roger is getting along with his new housekeeper?

At this Uncle Roger said with a wink, "The only problem I have with my new housekeeper is that she's so large I spend too much time walking around her." We all laughed until Aunt Janet rebuked him for being ungrateful for the Widow Hawkins' good housekeeping abilities. Aunt Janet continued reading:

Robert has a thriving practice, and I go with him at least once a week to help our neighbors in the areas that have no doctors. The people are so sweetly appreciative of Robert's medical care. Some of the women have new babies, and I'm enjoying helping them learn to care for their little ones. I've begun a little "Care and Share" shop here in our home, where we collect items that are needed. We take these with us each week when we visit the outlying areas. Robert is teaching me to

help him with simple nursing skills, and we find it such a joy to work together.

We think of each of you often, particularly our Story Girl. I miss her so much, but I'm sure she is enjoying living with all of her cousins. I do miss you too, dear Janet, and so far have not found a friend as loving and thoughtful as you. Just now the tears are coming to my eyes as I think of each of you.

Peter, I cannot tell you what it meant when Roger wrote that you will now be able to go to school full time. How exciting! I feel that you have great promise and expect to hear great things about you.

Cecily, dear, please take care of yourself, and always wear your warm coat and mittens and boots. You are precious to us.

Dear Felicity, I'm enclosing a bit of money for your birthday and hope you had a lovely day. I can hardly believe that you are thirteen already!

Dan, I know you and Alan's boys, Bev and Felix, are good friends, and I'm sure that you are all helping Alec and Roger with the farms. I really must go now and see that our cook has things in order for dinner. Please know that I love all of you and miss you terribly. Perhaps next Christmas the whole family can make the trip over here to be *with us. Robert's family is wonderful to me, but there is none like your own precious family, of course.*

> *With much love and prayer,*
> *Olivia*

As Aunt Janet finished reading, she folded the letter carefully and wiped her eyes on the tip of her apron. All of us sat with our own thoughts, missing Aunt Olivia so much. Dear Cecily could not keep a little sob from escaping as the tears began to roll down her cheeks.

"Isn't it always hard when you hear from ones you love so much?" asked the Story Girl. "From the picture I have of my mother, I know that Aunt Olivia looks a lot like her."

"Yes, she does, Sara," agreed Uncle Roger. "And she has the same sweet nature your mother had."

Aunt Olivia had been like a mother to her, and the sadness of having her so far away was overwhelming. Suddenly Sara jumped up, and with a muffled "Excuse me," raced up the stairs. She didn't cry often, but we knew the letter was just a bit too much.

Even Uncle Roger, always a tease, said he missed Olivia nagging him. All of us laughed at that, for Aunt Olivia was far too sweet to nag. We noticed that since Aunt Olivia had gone there was a real spark missing in Uncle Roger's household.

"Well, Roger, maybe you need more than a plump housekeeper," teased Uncle Alec. "If it's her nagging you miss, you may have to get yourself a wife."

"Oh, no you don't," said our bachelor uncle. "I haven't come to that point yet."

"How about making some fudge?" suggested Felicity, who thought good or bad times were always better with food.

"Sounds good to me if you girls stir it," said Dan.

"Come on, Cece. Wipe your tears, and let's get busy mixing it up," said Felicity. "I'll run upstairs and get the Story Girl, if you'll get the ingredients out."

While the girls started on the fudge, the fellows and I sat around the fire trying to get over our lonesome feelings by telling jokes and sharing small talk.

"Did you hear that one of the Mawr boys said someone reported that a light was seen at the schoolhouse around midnight after the concert?" said Dan.

"You don't say," I replied, winking at the Story Girl, who had just come back downstairs with Felicity. "You don't suppose it's haunted, do you?" I said for Sara Stanley's benefit. Of course, no one else knew anything about our midnight escapade to recover her necklace.

She looked at me with the sparkle returning to her eyes. "Probably just some moonlight glinting off the tin roof," she offered teasingly.

"Don't tell Cecily, but Emmeline Frewen said she saw a lock of Cecily's hair in Cyrus Brisk's Bible last Sunday," said Felix.

"You've gotta be kidding. Doesn't that chump know when he's licked?" Dan asked.

"Guess not. His sister Flossie told me that he means to keep it forever and use it as a bookmark," I said.

"I'll steal it out of his Bible at Sunday school next week," asserted Dan.

"That's no good," said Felix. "That would be stealing, and you know that Cecily wouldn't want you to steal."

"Well, Cyrus stole it from her," responded Dan.

"I know, but Pastor Marwood says two wrongs never make a right," Felix said.

"Guess you're right, but it just makes me mad as fire, and I ain't over it yet," said Cecily's outraged brother.

"Did ya hear that ole Billy Robinson got kicked by a cow last week?" asked Felix.

"Serves him right," said Peter. "He's so nasty to everybody."

"Especially me," sputtered Felix. "I'll never get over him selling me that phony Magic Seed last

41

summer. I still can't believe I was so stupid to believe him and lose that money."

"Not only you, Felix," soothed Peter. "About ten others believed him and lost money too. What a ninny he is."

"No sense crying over spilled milk, boys," advised Uncle Roger. "Just don't let it happen again. He's following the ways of his kinfolk, and they're a bad lot, I'm afraid. You boys have been taught better than to cheat and steal."

We knew he was right, but we still didn't like Billy and his ways. It was a good thing our uncles wouldn't allow us to be bitter and talk about people. We already did a fair amount of it when they weren't around to hear and rebuke us.

Just then Felicity came out of the pantry with a huge pan of fudge. "Come and get it, everyone."

She didn't have to call us twice. Things always sweetened up a bit when our girl cousins brought out the goodies. It wasn't long before we all said a "sweet" good night and headed upstairs to bed. There were some interesting whispered conversations before we fell asleep. We had been greatly impressed with Aunt Olivia's letter that showed what a fine husband she had.

"Boy! I hope I can find a good wife like Aunt Olivia," said Felix. "I guess I'll have to go on a diet before I'll find one who will have me."

"You'll just have to decide which you want more—fudge or a nice wife," I remarked.

"It's a hard choice," my brother muttered, rolling over with a sigh before falling asleep.

Peg Bowen Comes to Church

*Peg listened quietly until Mr. Davidson
was about halfway through his message
on the love of God. Suddenly she got to
her feet and said, "This is too dull for me.
I want something more exciting."*

Chapter Four

As I sit here writing about those days when we were children on the farms at Prince Edward Island, memories come flooding in. It's almost as though only a few days have gone by. I can remember the exact things we were doing and what I thought at the time.

I will never forget the time we bought "God's picture" from Jerry Cowan for fifty cents. Or the time Dan ate the poison berries. I laugh thinking about the time we heard the ghostly bell ring, the visit of the governor's wife, and the night we got lost in the blizzard. But none of those stand out in my mind more than the day Peg Bowen came to church and sat in our pew. It seems very funny to me now, but we didn't think it was a laughing matter at the time—far from it. Just ask Felicity.

It was a Sunday evening in July. Aunt Janet had one of her headaches, so she had to stay home. Uncle Alec decided to stay with her since her headaches sometimes made her feel dizzy and ill.

We "small fry," as Aunt Janet called us, walked together to church. We were dressed in our Sunday best and tried very hard to be on our best behavior as well. Those walks to church were fun for us. Peter and the Story Girl were always full of some new story or joke. We never hurried, always leaving in time to enjoy each other and not be late.

This particular evening was beautiful. It had been very hot during the day but cooled down as evening approached. The wheat fields all about us were ripening for harvest. The wind gossiped with the grasses along our way, and the buttercups danced along the road. Waves of shadows swept over the ripe hay fields. Bees sang happily as they buzzed over neighboring wayside gardens.

"The world is so lovely tonight," said the Story Girl. "I just hate the thought of going into the church and shutting all the sunlight and music outside. I wish we could have services outside in summer."

"I don't think that would be very religious," said Felicity.

"I'd feel ever so much more religious outside than in," responded the Story Girl.

"If the service were outside, we'd have to sit in the graveyard, and that wouldn't be very cheerful," said Felix.

"Besides, the music isn't shut out," added Felicity. "The choir is inside."

"Reverend Marwood is on vacation. I think we are having that young preacher—Mr. Davidson. Wonder how he'll be?" said Cecily.

"Guess we'll know when we hear him tonight," said Story Girl. "Uncle Roger says those who preach for the regular preachers while they're on vacation usually don't amount to much. He ought to be good. His uncle was a good preacher but terribly absent-minded. He used to be the minister in Baywater. He had a large family and his children were very mischievous. One day his wife was ironing and she ironed a great big nightcap with a frill around it. One of the preacher's children took the cap when the mother wasn't looking and hid it in his father's best hat—the one he wore on Sundays. When Mr. Davidson went to church the next Sunday he put his hat on without ever looking into the crown of the hat.

"He walked to church deep in thought on his message. At the door he took off his hat. The night-cap had slipped down on this head, just like it had been put on. The frill stood out around his face and he looked like a big baby. The strings hung down his back as if they were tied. As he walked down the aisle and up onto the platform, one of the elders saw him and tiptoed up and told him he had on his night cap.

"He reached up and grabbed it off in a dazed way and said, Bless me, it's Sally's nightcap. Now how do you suppose I could have gotten it on?'

"The whole congregation hooted with laughter, but old Mr. Davidson just stuffed it in his pocket and started the service. All the while he preached, the hat and its strings stuck out of his pocket."

"It seems to me," said Peter laughing, "that a funny story is funnier when it is about a minister than it is about any other man. I wonder why?"

"A good story is a good story—no matter who it is about," said the Story Girl firmly.

No one was at church when we reached it, so we took our accustomed walk through the graveyard. The Story Girl had brought flowers for her mother's grave as usual. While she arranged them on it, the rest of us read, for the umpteenth time, the epitaph on Great-Grandfather King's tombstone. The epitaph had been composed by Great-Grandmother King. It was famous among our famly as one of our traditions and we read it nearly every Sunday at church. The words were cut deeply in the slab of red Island sandstone and read as follows:

SWEET DEPARTED SPIRIT

Do receive the vows a grateful widow pays,
Each future day and night shall
hear her speak Isaac's praise.
Though thy beloved form must in the grave decay
Yet from her heart thy memory to time,
no change shall steal away.

Do thou from mansions of eternal bliss
remember thy distressed relict.
Look on her with an angel's love—soothe
her sad life and cheer her end
Through this world's dangers and its grief's.
Then meet her with thy
well-known smiles and welcome
At the last great day.

"I can't make out what the old lady was saying," said Dan with confusion.

"That's no way to speak of your great-grandmother," said Felicity with a rebuke.

"How does *The Family Guide* say you ought to speak of your great-grandma, *sweet one*?" asked Dan.

"Well, not as an *old lady*, Silliness," replied Felicity.

"There is one thing about it that puzzles me," reamarked Cecily. "She calls herself a *grateful* widow. Now what was she grateful for?"

"Maybe because she was rid of him at last," said Dan, with no tact at all.

"Oh, it couldn't have been that," protested Cecily seriously "I've always heard that Great-Grandfather and Great-Grandmother were very much in love with each other."

"Maybe, then, it means she was grateful that she'd had him as long as she did," suggested Peter.

"I think it means she was grateful because he had been so kind to her in life," said Felicity.

"What on earth is a *'distressed relict'*?" asked Felix.

"*'Relict'* is a word I hate," said Story Girl. "It sounds so much like relic. Relict means just the same as widow, only a man can be a relict, too."

"Great-grandmother seemed to run short of rhymes at the last of the epitaph," commented Dan.

"Finding rhymes isn't as easy as you might think," said Peter, remembering the difficulty he'd had writing the birthday ode for Felicity.

"I think Great-Grandmother King intended the last of the epitaph to be in blank verse," said Felicity with dignity.

"Well, it's *blank* to me," retorted Dan. "Why can't they just put the names of the dead on the tombstone and leave it at that?"

"Because they want to honor their dead by saying kind things about them," answered the Story Girl, who had just come from arranging the flowers on her mother's grave. "I'm so pleased that they wrote an epitaph for my mother. Come and see," she invited. There was still plenty of time before church, so we all walked a few feet away from Great-Grandfather King's plot to where the Story Girl's mother, our aunt Felicity, lay buried.

We had all seen Aunt Felicity's grave before.

"I only wish I could have known Mother," said the Story Girl softly, bending over to rearrange the pretty bunch of violets she had placed on her grave. "I was so young. I'm sorry to say that I can't remember her at all."

"I'm sure she was as lovely as you," said Peter. With that, we thoughtfully went into the church.

There were only a few people in the church when we went in and took our places in the old-fashioned, square King pew. We were just getting settled when Felicity said in a nervous whisper, "Look, here comes Peg Bowen!"

We all stared at Peg, who was coming slowly up the aisle. We may be excused for staring, for seldom did such a character invade the church. Peg was dressed in her usual short skirt, rather worn and frayed around the bottom. She had on her blouse of brilliant turkey-red calico. She wore no hat, and her stringy black hair streamed all over her shoulders. Her face and arms and feet were bare. But as bad as that might seem, they were covered with white *flour*. No one who saw her that evening would ever forget her.

Peg's black eyes looked wilder than usual that evening. She searched every pew until her eyes found us and then stopped by our pew.

"Spread out," whispered Felicity in desperation to us. "Make her think our pew is full!"

But Felicity was too late with her warning. The only result in our moving over was that she left a vacant spot between Felicity and the Story Girl, and Peg promptly plumped down in it.

"Well, I'm here," Peg said in a loud voice. "I did say once that I would never darken the door of the Carlisle Church again. I thought maybe I'd better come once in a while just to be on the safe side."

The poor girls were in agony. Everybody in the church was looking at our pew and smiling. We all felt that we were terribly disgraced. But we could do nothing. Peg was enjoying herself hugely. From where she sat, she could see the whole church, including the pulpit and balcony. Her restless eyes darted all over the place.

"Bless me, there's Sam Kinnaird," she exclaimed, out loud. "He's the man that dunned Jacob Marr for four cents on the church steps one Sunday. I heard him. He said, 'I think, Jacob, you still owe me four cents on that cow you bought last fall. I really need you to pay up.' It was so funny 'cause the Kinnairds were all mighty rich. I guess that's how they got rich.

"And there's Melita Ross," went on Peg. "She's got the same bonnet on she had last time I was in Carlisle Church six years ago. Some folks have the knack of making things last.

54

"But would ye look at the style Mrs. Elmer Brewer wears?" she went on. "Ye would never know her mother died in the poorhouse, would ye?

"Here comes old Stephen Grant," said Peg viciously, shaking her floury fist at him. "Look at him acting like butter wouldn't melt in his mouth. He may be an elder, but he's a scoundrel just the same. He set fire to his house to git the insurance fer it and then blamed *me*. Oh, yes, he knows that— and so do I. Hee! Hee!"

Peg chuckled fiendishly, and Stephen Grant tried to look as if nothing had been said.

"Oh, will the minister never come?" moaned Felicity in my ear. "Surely she'll have to stop then."

But the minister didn't come, and Peg had no intention of stopping.

"And there's Timothy Patterson—the meanest man alive—meaner than Sam Kinnaird even. Timothy pays his children five cents apiece to go without their suppers. Then he steals the cents out of their pockets after they've gone to bed. It's a fact. And when his old father died, he wouldn't let his wife put the old man's best shirt on him. He said a second-best shirt was plenty good to be buried in. That's another fact."

"I can't stand much more of this," wailed Felicity.

"See here, Miss Bowen, you really shouldn't talk like that about people," said Peter, trying to get her to be quiet.

"Bless ye, boy," said Peg. "The only difference between me and other folks is that I say these things out loud, and they just think them. If I told ye all the things I know about people in this church, ye'd be amazed. How about a peppermint?"

To our horror, Peg pulled a handful of dirty peppermints from the pocket of her skirt and handed one to each of us. "Eat them," she commanded.

We held them gingerly in our fingers, and then I said, "We aren't allowed to eat candy in church, Miss Bowen."

"Well, I've seen ladies and gents just as fine as ye eat peppermints in church," she said in an offended way. She popped a peppermint into her mouth and sucked it noisily. *At least she isn't talking while she sucks on it,* I thought with relief.

"Look at Dave Erskine strutting in," she went on. "They say the Lord made everybody, but I believe the Devil made all the Erskines."

"She's getting worse all the time. What will she say next?" whispered Felicity.

But our agony was over at last. The minister appeared in the pulpit, and Peg shushed. She folded her bare floury arms over her chest and fastened her black eyes on the young preacher. Her behavior for the next half hour was good, except when the minister prayed that we might be loving in our judgment and behavior. Peg said "Amen" two or three times very loudly and forcibly. Peg was a stranger to the visiting preacher. When she said her "amens," he opened his eyes and looked at our pew in a startled way.

Peg listened quietly until Mr. Davidson was about halfway through his message on the love of God. Suddenly she got to her feet and said, "This is too dull for me. I want something more exciting."

Mr. Davidson stopped short, and the congregation let out a collective gasp as Peg marched down the aisle. Halfway down, she turned around and faced the minister.

"There are so many hypocrites in this church that it isn't fit for decent people to come to," she said. "I won't be back!"

Wheeling around, she strode to the door, then stopped and sent off a parting shot. "I've felt kind of worried for God sometimes, seeing he has so much to attend to," she said. "But I see I needn't be so worried as long as there's plenty of ministers to tell him what to do."

With that Peg shook the dust of the Carlisle Church from her feet and went on her way. Poor Mr. Davidson began his sermon again, but he had a hard time getting it together. Certainly the congregation found it difficult to listen. Most of them were thinking about all of the things Peg had to say about them. We cousins couldn't even remember the Scripture text when we got home.

Felicity could not be comforted. "Now Mr. Davidson will surely think Peg is one of our family," she said bitterly. "Oh, I feel as if I could never get over such a mortification, Peter. I do wish you wouldn't go telling people they ought to go to church like you told Peg. It's all your fault that this happened."

"I never did think the church was just for God's people," said Peter defensively. "I thought church was where people could go to feel loved and find God's help, even though they don't know how to behave."

"You're right, Peter. Poor Peg is a lost soul. Maybe we'll have another opportunity to help her. Anyway, this is one day we will always remember," said the Story Girl.

She got that right. We never forgot the Sunday Peg Bowen came to church.

The Opening of the Blue Chest

Uncle Alec brought in the ax and used it to pry off the cover of the old blue chest, while everybody stood around in silence.

Chapter Five

T he day was dreary with threatening rain clouds hovering overhead. We cousins had drooped around all day with nothing particular to do. I guess we must have been in Aunt Janet's way, because she suggested that we go to the post office and get the mail.

When we arrived back at the farmhouse, Aunt Janet settled down at the kitchen table to read the mail, while we stood around eating our candy.

"Well, can you believe this!" Aunt Janet said, holding up a letter from Montreal for us to see. "This letter is from James Ward's wife in Montreal. Rachel Ward is dead. Jim's wife says she wants me to open the old blue chest."

"Hurrah!" said Dan, dancing a jig.

"Daniel King," said his mother severely. "Rachel Ward was your relation, and she is dead. What do you mean by such behavior?"

"I didn't know her," said Dan, sulking. "And I wasn't saying 'hurrah' because she is dead. I said 'hurrah' because the blue chest is to be opened at last. All of the girls complain every time they have to move it to wash and wax the floor. So hurrah! Now we can find out what's in it."

"So poor Rachel is gone," said Uncle Alec, walking over to the old chest that was against the wall in the kitchen. Sitting down on it, he ran his hand over it lovingly. "Rachel must have been an old woman—seventy-five, I guess. I remember her as a fine lovely young woman. Well, well—so the old chest is to be opened at last. How sad to think that all these years her things have been locked away, all because she was jilted on her wedding day. What are we supposed to do with all her stuff?"

"Rachel left a letter to James's wife telling about them," Aunt Janet replied. "The wedding dress and veil and letters are to be burned. There are two jugs that are to be sent to James's wife. The rest of the things are to be given to members of the family. Each is to have one item to remember her by."

"Oh, can't we open it right away this very night?" said Felicity eagerly.

"No indeed!" said Aunt Janet, folding up the letter. "The chest has been locked up for fifty years. We can stand to leave it locked up one more night. You children wouldn't sleep a wink if we opened it now. You'd be too excited."

"I'm sure I won't sleep anyhow," said Felicity. "You'll at least open it first thing in the morning, won't you, Ma?"

"No, I'll do nothing of the sort," was Aunt Janet's answer. "I want to get the work out of the way first— and Roger will want to be here. We'll say tomorrow around ten o'clock."

"That's sixteen whole hours to wait," sighed Felicity.

Cecily ran down the hill to tell Sara Ray, and the Story Girl ran over to tell Uncle Roger and Peter. We were all excited and spent the evening talking about the contents of the chest. That night Cecily dreamed that moths had gotten into it and eaten everything.

The morning dawned on a beautiful foggy world. There was just enough fog to look like a filmy veil of lace hanging on the dark evergreen trees. All of us sat around that morning impatiently watching the clock. "It seems like ten o'clock will never come," sighed the Story Girl. "The work is all done, and everybody is already here. We might as well open the chest right now."

"Mother *said* ten o'clock, and she'll stick to it," said Felicity crossly. "It's only nine now."

"Let's set the clock up half an hour," said the Story Girl impishly. "The clock in the hall isn't running, so no one will know the difference."

We all looked at each other.

"I wouldn't dare," said Felicity fearfully.

"Oh, I'll do it," said the Story Girl.

When ten o'clock struck, Aunt Janet came into the kitchen.

"There now, that didn't seem so long, did it," she remarked innocently. We must have looked awfully guilty, but none of the grown-ups suspected anything. Uncle Alec brought in the ax and used it to pry off the cover of the old blue chest, while everybody stood around in silence.

Then came the unpacking. It sure was interesting. Aunt Janet and Uncle Alec took everything out and laid each item on the kitchen table. We children were forbidden to touch anything, but at least we could see and talk.

"There are the pink and gold vases Grandmother King gave her," said Felicity as Aunt Janet unwrapped them from their pink paper. They were lovely, slender, old-fashioned, thin pink glass vases with gold leaves scattered over them. "Aren't they handsome?"

"Look," exclaimed Cecily delightedly, "there's the china fruit basket with the apple on the handle. Doesn't it look real? I've thought so much about it. Oh, Mother, please let me hold it for a minute. I'll be as careful as I can."

Following these, there were the two jugs to be sent to James's wife and an old antique candlestick of blue china.

"They are handsome," said Aunt Janet a bit enviously. "They must be a hundred years old. Aunt Sara Ward gave them to Rachel, and she had them for at least fifty years. I should have thought one would have been enough for James's wife. But, of course, we must do just as Rachel wanted."

"I declare, look at these tin muffin pans! They are still shiny and pretty," said Felicity.

"Here are her quilts," said Uncle Alec. "Yes, there is the blue and white bedspread Grandmother Ward gave her and the Rising Sun quilt her aunt Nancy made. I remember when they made them. And look at the braided rug. Why, the colors aren't faded one bit. I would like that rug, Janet."

Underneath the linens were Rachel Ward's wedding clothes. The girls were beside themselves with excitement over them. There was a beautiful shawl still in the wrappings from some fancy store and a long scarf of yellowed lace. There was the embroidered petticoat and many pairs of undies with handmade lace that caused the girls to blush. The fashions of Rachel's day were much fancier than ours.

"This was her 'going away' dress," said Aunt Janet, lifting out a long green silk dress. "It's full of moth holes, but what a pretty color it was! Look at the skirt, girls. How many yards must be in it? Hoopskirts were in then."

"Where is her wedding hat, Mama?" asked Cecily in a disappointed voice.

"I don't see it, Cecily," answered Aunt Janet. "I was told that she packed it away too, but she couldn't have. It certainly isn't here. I have heard that the white feather on it cost a small fortune. Here is her black silk cape. It seems terrible to meddle with these clothes that were so precious to her."

"Don't be foolish," said Uncle Alec, who wasn't sentimental where women's clothes were concerned. "They must be unpacked, at least. And then they must be burned. Only the purple dress doesn't have holes. It could be made over nicely for you, Felicity," he said in a practical way.

"No, thank you," said Felicity with a little shudder. "I would feel like a ghost. Make it over for yourself, Mother."

"Well, I will, if you don't want it. I'm not troubled by nerves. This must be the wedding dress," she said, lifting it out carefully.

"Oh," breathed the girls, crowding close to her as she cut the cord around the box. Inside was a lovely wedding dress of soft silk that had once been white. It was now yellowed with age. Folded around the dress was a long wedding veil. As Aunt Janet lifted it out, there was a strange, old-time perfume that had kept its sweetness all these years.

"Poor Rachel Ward," said the Story Girl softly. "All of her dreams have been locked in this old, blue chest."

"Here is her lace handkerchief. She made it herself. It's as fine as a spider's web. And . . . here are the letters Will Montague wrote to her. And this must be their picture," she said, taking up a red velvet case with a tarnished gold clasp. Looking out at us was the handsome Will and Rachel herself, with a shy wistful smile.

"Why, Rachel Ward wasn't a bit pretty!" exclaimed the Story Girl in disappointment.

"At last! A heroine who isn't pretty!" exclaimed Dan.

No, Rachel Ward wasn't pretty. That was a fact. The picture showed a fresh young face, plain and homely, with large black eyes and black curls hanging around the shoulders in old-time style.

"Rachel wasn't pretty," agreed Uncle Alec, "but she had a lovely color and a beautiful smile. She looks sad in that picture."

"Perhaps she knew that Will didn't really love her," said the Story Girl, who could sense a story anywhere.

"But how awful of him not to show up at the church. How could she ever bear to face their friends and family?" asked the prideful Felicity.

"She had a strength of character, Felicity," said Aunt Janet softly. "She just went in the house, took off her wedding dress, and packed all of her things away. I'm sure she cried in the night, but no one ever heard her. She never spoke of Will again. That evening she helped serve the guests who had come from a distance for the wedding. She was so lovely in her sorrow. Everyone dearly loved and respected her for it."

"He was a handsome one," growled Uncle Alec, taking the picture and looking at it. "But I never liked him. I was only a little boy of ten, and yet I saw through him. Rachel Ward was far too good for him."

"May we read the letters?" asked Cecily eagerly.

"Oh, no, dear," answered Aunt Janet. "They were for Rachel's eyes only. They must be burned now along with the wedding dress. Their memories are too private for any of us to read." Aunt Janet took the wedding dress and veil, the picture case, and the letters to burn. The rest of the things were put back in the chest.

While Aunt Janet was gone the clock was reset before our grown-ups were any the wiser. Peter stayed for supper that night, and we made taffy in the kitchen.

As the Story Girl was stirring the candy, she said, "Of course it was interesting to see the old chest unpacked. But now that it's over, I believe I'm sorry it's opened. It isn't mysterious any longer. I just love mysteries."

"I guess I do too if they end nicely. I guess they didn't end very well for poor Rachel Ward," said Cecily.

"No, but Aunt Olivia told me that she led a happy life even though she was disappointed in love," said the Story Girl. "She became a teacher and was dearly loved by all of the children in her school and her family. I guess it just proves that you can be happy and useful no matter what may come to pass."

"Yep!" answered Peter. "If life hands you a lemon, you just make lemonade."

"That makes me thirsty," laughed Felicity. "I don't have any lemons, but we can have raspberry punch and cookies."

"Felicity, you are a wonder," said Peter, looking at his beloved with stars in his eyes.

"Yeah! You *wonder* what she is," said her feisty brother, Dan.

"Watch it, Dan, or you will *wonder* where your punch and cookies are," snapped Felicity.

Once again we were spared a brother and sister quarrel by the prospect of excellent refreshments. If Felicity could do one thing well, it was fix the eats.

The Missionary Heroine

*Mr. Campbell scowled at us. "Stuff and
nonsense!" he yelled angrily. "I don't
believe in foreign missions. I don't believe
in them at all. I never give a cent to them.
It's all just a scam to get money."*

Chapter Six

It was a glorious August afternoon, and we six King cousins were sitting around the Pulpit Stone in the orchard with Miss Reade. She was living up to her "Beautiful Alice" name that day—dressed in a thin blue organdy dress and a droopy hat that protected her lovely skin from the sun. She had been up to give the girls their music lessons, and, indeed, she was so beautiful that it almost made us fellows consider taking lessons as well.

While we were talking, the sun glinted, and I noticed a sparkle on her finger. The twinkle came from a large, handsome sapphire ring. It was not a new ring but was a lovely old-fashioned design with small diamonds clustered around the larger blue stone.

Once Miss Reade had gone, I asked the Story Girl if she had noticed the ring. She nodded but said no more about it.

"Look here, Sara," I said, "there's something about that ring—and you know what it is."

"I told you once there was a story growing, but you would have to wait until it was fully grown," she answered.

"Is Miss Reade going to marry? Someone we know?" I persisted.

"Curiosity killed the cat," observed the Story Girl coolly. "Miss Reade hasn't told me that she is planning to marry. We will all find out in due time."

When the Story Girl put on grown-up airs like that, I didn't admire her so much, and I dropped the subject with a dignity that seemed to amuse her.

Our Cecily had been faithfully working on the large quilt square she was embroidering for her missionary project at church. She had been busy collecting names for it ever since the autumn before, and she now had a great many. Kitty Marr had one more than Cecily, and this was certainly something that bothered our little cousin.

"Besides, one I've got isn't even paid for—Peg Bowen's," Cecily said. "And I don't suppose it ever will be, for I'll never dare ask her for it."

"I wouldn't put her name on the quilt at all," said Felicity.

"Oh, I don't dare not to. She would be sure to find out and be very angry. I wish I could get just one more name though. Then I would be content. But I don't know of a single person that hasn't been asked already."

"Except Mr. Campbell," said Dan.

"Oh, of course. Nobody would *dare* ask Mr. Campbell. We all know it would be of no use. He doesn't believe in missions at all—in fact, he says he detests the very mention of missionaries and never gives one cent to any of them."

"All the same, I think he ought to be asked so that he doesn't have the excuse that no one *asked* him," declared Dan.

"Do you really think so, Dan?" asked Cecily.

"Sure," said Dan solemnly. Cecily looked thoughtful and concerned for the rest of the day. The next morning she came to me and said, "Bev, would you like to go for a walk with me this afternoon?"

"Of course," I replied. "Any particular place you want to go?"

"I'm going to see Mr. Campbell and ask him if I may embroider his name on my quilt," said Cecily. "I don't suppose it will do any good. He wouldn't give anything to the library last summer, you remember, until the Story Girl told him that story about his grandmother. She won't go with me this time.

"I don't know why I'm so afraid of him. He's just a man, but I'm frightened to death at the very thought. I do believe, however, that it is my duty. And besides, I would love to get as many names for my quilt as Kitty Marr. So if you are willing, we can go this afternoon. I simply *couldn't* go alone."

That afternoon we took a walk together, and in spite of the fact that we didn't expect the interview to be a very pleasant one, we enjoyed our time anyway.

To be sure, Mr. Campbell had been quite nice to us the last time we called on him. But the Story Girl had been with us and had coaxed him into a good humor and generous attitude with her magical voice and personality. We didn't have that help with us now, and Mr. Campbell was known to be terribly opposed to missions in any shape or form.

"It might have helped if I had worn my best dress," Cecily said, glancing down at her old print dress. It was neat and clean but rather faded, short, and tight. "The Story Girl said it would be better if I could wear prettier clothes, but Mother wouldn't let me. She said it was all nonsense and that Mr. Campbell would never notice what I had on."

"It's my opinion that Mr. Campbell notices a good deal more than you think," I said wisely.

"Well, I wish our visit was over," sighed Cecily. "I can't tell you how much I dread it."

"Now, look here, Cece," I said cheerfully, "let's not think about it until we get there. It will only spoil our walk and do no good. Let's just forget it and enjoy ourselves."

"I'll try," agreed Cecily, "but it's a lot easier to 'preach what to do than to practice it.'"

It was Mr. Campbell's housekeeper who came to the door, and she ushered us into the sitting room where Mr. Campbell was reading. He laid down his book with a frown and said nothing at all in response to our timid "Good afternoon." But after we had been sitting for a few moments in terrible silence, wishing ourselves a thousand miles away, he said with a chuckle, "Well, is it the school library again?"

Cecily had remarked as we were coming that what she dreaded most of all was introducing the subject. But Mr. Campbell had given her a splendid opening, and she plunged wildly in at once, rattling off her explanation with a trembling voice and flushed cheeks.

"No, it's our missionary group's quilt, Mr. Campbell. There are to be as many squares in it as there are members in our group. Each member has a large square and is collecting names to embroider on it. If you want to have your name on a square, you pay five cents. If you want to have it right in the round spot in the middle of the square, you must pay ten cents. The money is to go to the little girl our missionary group is supporting in Korea. I heard that no one had asked you, so I thought that perhaps you might give me your name for my square."

Mr. Campbell scowled at us. "Stuff and nonsense!" he yelled angrily. "I don't believe in foreign missions. I don't believe in them at all. I never give a cent to them. It's all just a scam to get money."

"Five cents isn't a very large amount of money," said Cecily bravely.

Mr. Campbell's scowl disappeared, and he laughed. "It wouldn't break me," he admitted, "but it's the principle of the thing. And as for that mission band of yours, if it weren't for the fun you get out of it, not one of you would belong to it. You don't really care a cent more for the heathen than I do."

"Oh, no, we certainly do care!" protested Cecily. "We do think of all the poor children in Korea. We like to think we are helping them, even if only a little. We *are* in earnest, Mr. Campbell. Indeed we are."

"I don't believe it. Don't believe a word of it," said Mr. Campbell impolitely. "Oh, you'll do things that are nice and interesting. You'll plan concerts and chase people about for autographs and give money that your poor parent's give to you.

"But you wouldn't do anything that costs you time or effort. You wouldn't do anything that you disliked for the heathen children, or you wouldn't make any real sacrifice for them, would you?"

"Indeed we would," cried Cecily, forgetting her fear. "I just wish I had a chance to prove it to you."

"You do, huh? Come on now. I'll take you at your word. I'll test you. Tomorrow is Communion Sunday, and the church will be full. Everyone will be wearing their very best clothes. Go to church tomorrow in the very dress that you have on now, without telling anyone why you are doing it until it is all over, and I'll give you five dollars for that quilt of yours."

Poor Cecily! To go to church in a faded print dress with a shabby old sun hat and worn shoes! It was very cruel of Mr. Campbell.

"I don't think Mother would let me," she faltered.

Her tormenter smiled at her. "It's not hard to find some excuse," he said sarcastically.

Cecily turned red and sat up facing Mr. Campbell spunkily.

"It's *not* an excuse," she said. "If Mother will let me go to church like this, I'll do it. But I'll have to tell her why, Mr. Campbell. I am certain she will never let me wear this old dress unless I do."

"Oh, you can tell all your own family," said Mr. Campbell. "But remember, no one can tell anyone at church until Sunday is over. If they do, I'll be sure to find it out, and our bargain will be off. If I see you in church tomorrow dressed as you are now, I will give you my name and five dollars. But I won't see you. You'll shrink when you've had time to think it over."

"I will not," said Cecily.

"Well, we'll see. And now come to the barn with me. I have the prettiest little calves out there you have ever seen. I want you to see them."

Mr. Campbell took us all over his barns and was very kind. He had beautiful horses, cows, and sheep, and I enjoyed seeing them. I don't think Cecily did, however. She was very quiet, and even Mr. Campbell's handsome, new gray horse failed to interest her. She was already thinking about tomorrow and how she would get through it. On the way home she asked me seriously if I thought Mr. Campbell would go to heaven when he died.

"Of course he will," I said. "Isn't he a member of the church?"

"Oh yes, but just being a church member isn't all it takes. I can't imagine him fitting into heaven. You know, he isn't really fond of anything but livestock. He surely won't have much reason to be there."

"He's fond of teasing people," I responded. "None of us can ever know anybody's heart. Perhaps you'll have an opportunity to talk to him about it sometime, Sis."

Cecily never responded when I said that, but her eyes were huge just thinking about approaching Mr. Campbell with such a delicate notion as whether he was going to heaven. I decided to change the subject quickly. •

"Are you really going to church tomorrow in that dress, Sis?"

"If Mother let's me, I'll have to," said poor Cecily. "I don't want to let Mr. Campbell get the best of me, and I *do* want to have as many names as possible for my quilt. But it will be simply dreadful. I don't know whether I hope Mother will let me or not."

I didn't believe Aunt Janet would let her go to church in that old dress, but sometimes our aunt could be depended on to do the unexpected. She laughed and told Cecily that she could please herself. Felicity was in a rage over it and declared that she wouldn't go to church if Cecily went in such a rag of a dress. Dan sarcastically said if all she went to church for was to show off her fine clothes and look at other people's, then it was no good going at all.

I think Cecily wished it might rain the next day, but it was beautiful. We were all waiting in the orchard for the Story Girl, who was late getting dressed. Felicity was in her prettiest flower-trimmed hat, a crisp muslin dress with floating ribbons, and trim black slippers. Poor Cecily stood beside her, pale and silent in her faded school garb and heavy copper-toed boots. But her face, if pale, was also determined. Cecily having "put her hand to the plow" was not one to turn back.

"You do look just awful," said Felicity. "I don't care—I am going to sit in Mr. Dale's pew. I *won't* sit with you. There will be so many strangers there and all the Markdale people. What will they think? Some of them will never know the reason you're dressed that way."

"I wish the Story Girl would hurry," was all poor Cecily said. "We're going to be late. It wouldn't have been quite so hard if I could have gotten there before everyone else and slipped quietly into our pew."

"Here comes the Story Girl at last," said Dan. "Why—what's she got on?"

The Story Girl joined us with a quizzical smile on her face. Dan whistled. Cecily's pale cheeks flushed with understanding and gratitude. The Story Girl had on her school print dress, no gloves, and her old heavy school shoes.

"You're not going to have to go through this all alone, Cecily," she said.

"Oh, it won't be half so hard now," said Cecily, smiling at the Story Girl with appreciation.

I think it was hard enough even then. The Story Girl didn't care at all, but Cecily squirmed under the curious glances of the church people. She told me afterward that she didn't think she could have endured it at all if she had been alone.

Mr. Campbell met us under the elms in the church-yard with a twinkle in his eye. "Well, you did it, Miss Cecily," he said, "but you didn't exactly follow the rules, since your friend Sara Stanley helped you out by dressing in her old clothes too. You should have been alone. I suppose you think you cheated me nicely."

"No, she doesn't," spoke up the Story Girl. "She was all dressed and ready to come before she knew I was dressed this way. She kept her part of the bargain, Mr. Campbell, and I think you were cruel to make her do it."

"You do, huh? Well, I hope you will forgive me. I didn't think for a moment that she would do it. I was sure that girlish pride would win the day over her missionary heart. It seems I was wrong—though we will never know how much was missionary zeal and how much was plain King spunk. I'll keep my promise, Miss King. You will have your five dollars, and don't forget to put my name in the round space. No five-cent corners for me."

Cecily sat in church that morning with a sweet smile on her face. She had accomplished what she had set out to do—fill her missionary quilt with more names than anyone else. At the same time, she had proven an important point to Mr. Campbell.

Jasper Dale's Exciting News

"Mrs. Griggs says that the room
has been locked for ten years. Ten years
ago Miss Reade was just a little girl
of ten. She *couldn't* be the 'Alice'
of the books," argued Felicity.

Chapter Seven

"I'll have something exciting to tell you this evening," said the Story Girl at breakfast one morning. Her eyes were very bright and excited. She had spent the evening before with Miss Reade and had not returned until the rest of us were in bed. Miss Reade had finished giving music lessons and was going home to Charlottetown in a few days. Cecily and Felicity were very sad about this, but the Story Girl, who had seemed even more devoted to Miss Reade than they, hadn't expressed any regret and seemed quite cheerful about the whole matter.

"Why can't you tell us *now*?" questioned Felicity.

"Because the evening is the nicest time to tell things. I only mentioned it now so that you would have something interesting to look forward to all day."

"Is it about Miss Reade?" asked Cecily.

"Never mind."

"I'll bet she's getting married," I exclaimed, remembering the ring that I had seen.

The Story Girl gave me an annoyed look. She didn't like anyone "stealing her thunder" when she had a story to tell.

"I'm not saying it's about Miss Reade or it isn't," she said. "You must just wait until this evening."

"I wonder what it is?" questioned Cecily as the Story Girl left the room.

"I don't believe it's much of anything," said Felicity, beginning to clear away the breakfast dishes. "The Story Girl likes to make so much out of so little. Anyhow, I don't believe Miss Reade is getting married. She doesn't have any suitors around here, and Mrs. Armstrong says she's sure that she doesn't write to anyone. Besides, if she were, she wouldn't be likely to tell the Story Girl."

"Oh, she might. They're good friends, you know," said Cecily.

"Miss Reade is no better friends with her than she is with me and you," retorted Felicity.

"No, but sometimes it seems to me that she is a different kind of friend with the Story Girl than she is with me and you."

"Such nonsense," snipped Felicity.

"It's only some girl secrets," said Dan. "I don't have much interest in it."

But he was on hand with the rest of us that evening, interest or no interest. We sat in Uncle Steven's Walk, where the glorious trees drooped with sweet fragrance and fruit. The apples looked like jewels on the boughs of the trees.

"Now are you going to tell us your news?" asked Felicity impatiently.

"Miss Reade *is* going to be married," said the Story Girl. "She told me so last night. She will be married in one month."

"Who to?" exclaimed the girls.

"To—to—to the Awkward Man."

For a few moments, all of us were struck dumb.

"Do you really mean it, Sara Stanley?" gasped Felicity.

"Indeed I do. I thought you'd be surprised. Do you remember that evening last spring when I went for a walk with Miss Reade? I told you when I came back that a story was growing. I guessed it from the way the Awkward Man looked at her when I stopped to speak to him over his garden fence."

"But—the Awkward Man!" said Felicity helplessly. "It doesn't seem possible. Did Miss Reade tell you *herself*?"

"Yes."

"I suppose it must be true then, but how did it ever come about? He's so shy and awkward. How did he ever manage to get up enough spunk to ask her to marry him?"

"Maybe she asked him," suggested Dan.

"Not exactly," Sara said.

"You might tell us what he said," urged Cecily. "We'd never tell."

The Story Girl shook her head. "No, I can't. You wouldn't understand. Besides, I couldn't tell it just right. I'd spoil it if I told it. Perhaps someday I will be able to tell it properly. It's very beautiful—but it might sound ridiculous if it isn't told the right way."

"I don't know what you mean, and I don't believe you know yourself," said Felicity. "All that I can make out is that Miss Reade is going to marry Jasper Dale, and I don't like the idea one bit. She is so beautiful and sweet. I thought she'd marry some dashing young man. Jasper Dale must be at least twenty years older, and he's practically a hermit."

"Miss Reade is perfectly happy. She thinks the Awkward Man is wonderful—and so he is. You don't know him like I do."

"Well, you needn't put on such airs about it," pouted Felicity.

"I'm not putting on any airs," said the Story Girl, "but it's true. Miss Reade and I are the only people in Carlisle who really know the Awkward Man. No one else ever got behind his shyness to find out just what sort of person he is."

"When are they to be married?" asked Felicity.

"In a month's time, and then after their honeymoon they are coming back here to live at Golden

Milestone. Won't it be lovely to have Miss Reade always so near?"

"I wonder what she'll think about the mystery of Golden Milestone," remarked Felicity.

Golden Milestone was the beautiful name the Awkward Man had given his home. Felicity was referring to a locked room at Golden Milestone that looked as if it had been prepared for some lady. It was completely furnished, and there were several books that were inscribed "To Alice." It had been a great mystery to all of us King cousins. We found out about it through Mr. Dale's housekeeper.

"She knows all about the mystery and thinks it's perfectly lovely, and so do I," said the Story Girl.

"Do you know the secret of the locked rooms?" cried Cecily.

"Yes, the Awkward Man told me all about it last night. I told you I'd find out the mystery one day."

"And what is it?"

"I can't tell you that either."

"I think you're hateful and mean," exclaimed Felicity. "It hasn't anything to do with Miss Reade, so I think you might as well tell us."

"It has something to do with Miss Reade, all right. It's all about her," said the Story Girl.

"Well, I don't see how that can be, when the Awkward Man never saw or heard of Miss Reade until she came to Carlisle in the spring," said Felicity. "And he's had that locked room for years."

"I can't explain it to you, but it's just as I've said," responded the Story Girl.

"Well, it's a very weird thing," said Felicity.

"The name in the books in the room was 'Alice,' and Miss Reade's name is Alice," muttered Cecily. "Did he know her before she came here?"

"Mrs. Griggs says the room has been locked for ten years. Ten years ago Miss Reade was just a little girl of ten. *She* couldn't be the 'Alice' of the books," argued Felicity.

"I wonder if she'll wear the blue silk dress," said Sara Ray. She was referring to a lovely blue silk dress that was thrown over the rocking chair in the room.

"And what will she do about the picture in the room if it isn't hers?" asked Cecily.

"The picture couldn't be hers, or Mrs. Griggs would have known her when she came to Carlisle," said Felix.

"I'm going to stop wondering about it," exclaimed Felicity crossly. She was aggravated by the Story Girl's amused smile. "I think Sara is just mean when she won't tell us."

"I can't," repeated the Story Girl patiently.

"You said one time that you had an idea who 'Alice' was," I said. "Was your idea right?"

"Yes. I guessed right."

"Do you suppose that they'll keep the room locked after they are married?" asked Cecily.

"Oh, no. I can tell you that much. It's to be Miss Reade's own sitting room."

I think Miss Reade is simply throwing herself away. But I hope she'll be happy. I hope the Awkward Man will manage to get married without some major blunder, which is more than anyone could expect.

"The ceremony is going to be very private," said the Story Girl.

"I hope I get to see them when they come to church after they're married," chuckled Dan. "I wonder how he'll ever manage to bring her to church and show her into the pew? I bet he'll go in first—or tramp on her dress—or fall over his feet."

Seeing the look on the Story Girl's face, I said, "What is the matter, Sara?"

"I hate to hear them talking like that about Miss Reade and Mr. Dale," she answered. "It's really all so beautiful, but they make it seem silly and absurd, somehow."

"You might tell me all about it, Sara. I wouldn't tell, and I'd understand."

"Yes, Bev, I think you would," she said thoughtfully. "But I can't tell it, even to you, because I can't tell it well enough yet. I sense that there's only one way to tell this story—and I don't know the way yet. Someday I'll know, and then I'll tell you, Bev."

A long, long time later she kept her word. It had been forty years when I wrote to her across the long distance that divided us and told her that Jasper Dale was dead. I reminded her of her old promise to tell me his story. In reply, she wrote out the love story of Jasper Dale and Alice Reade. Now, when Alice sleeps under the whispering trees of the old Carlisle churchyard beside the husband of her youth, that story may be given to the world in all its old-time sweetness.

The Awkward Man's Love Story

(Written by the Story Girl)

*"Jasper!" cried Alice, finding her voice.
His anger hurt her with a pain she couldn't
endure. It was unbearable that Jasper should
be angry with her. In that moment she
realized that she loved him.*

Chapter Eight

Jasper Dale had lived alone at Golden Milestone since his mother's death. He was twenty years old at the time. Now he was close to forty, though he didn't look it. It couldn't be said that he looked young either. He had never at anytime looked young. There had always been something in his appearance that stamped him as different from ordinary men. Apart from his shyness, a wall seemed to exist between him and other men. He had lived all his life in Carlisle. All of the Carlisle people thought they knew everything about him. But the only thing they really knew was that he was painfully shy.

Jasper never went anywhere except to church. He didn't take part in Carlisle's simple social life. He was distant and reserved even with men. As for women, he never spoke or looked at them. If a woman spoke to him, even if she were an old mother, he was at once in an agony of painful blushes. He had no friends in the sense of companions. To all outward appearances his life was quite solitary.

Mrs. Griggs, his housekeeper, who was very curious, explored the house from floor to attic in her cleaning binges. Her report of the condition was always the same—"neat as can be." To be sure, she wondered about one locked room, however, in the west gable that looked out on the garden and the pines in the yard. Mrs. Griggs knew that in the lifetime of Jasper Dale's mother it had been unfurnished. She supposed it remained so, though she always tried the door.

Jasper Dale had a good, well-cultivated farm. He had a large garden where he spent most of his spare time in the summer. It was supposed that he read a great deal since the postmistress declared that he was always getting books and magazines by mail. He seemed content with his existence, and people left him alone since that seemed to be the greatest kindness they could do for him. It was supposed that he would never marry.

But one day Mrs. Griggs left Golden Milestone with a strange story, which made for a good deal of gossip. Although people listened eagerly, many felt that Mrs. Griggs was crazy. Others thought her imagination had gone wild. Some felt that she had invented the whole story. Mrs. Griggs' story was as follows:

One day she found the door of the west wing of Jasper's house unlocked. She went in expecting to see bare walls and a collection of odds and ends. Instead she found herself in a finely furnished room with lovely thick carpet. Delicate lace curtains hung on the small square windows. The walls had many pictures, exhibiting fine taste. A bookcase filled with lovely leather-bound books stood between the windows. Beside the bookcase stood a worktable with a dainty basket on it. By the basket, she saw a pair of tiny scissors and a silver thimble.

A wicker rocker made comfortable with silk cushions stood nearby. Above the bookcase hung a woman's picture done in watercolor. The picture bore the image of a lovely lady with a pale sweet face. She had large dark eyes with a wistful expression under loose masses of shiny lustrous hair. Just beneath the picture on the top shelf of the bookcase was a vase full of flowers. Another vase of flowers stood beside the basket.

All of this was astonishing enough, but what puzzled Mrs. Griggs completely was a woman's dress—a pale blue silk dress—that was hanging over the chair before the mirror—and on the floor beside it were two blue satin slippers!

Good Mrs. Griggs didn't leave the room until she had thoroughly explored it, even to shaking out the blue dress. She discovered that it was a tea gown, "a wrapper," she called it. But she found nothing that would explain the mysterious furnishings. The fact that the simple name "Alice" was written on the flyleaf of all the books deepened the mystery. Alice was a name unknown in the Dale family.

Mrs. Griggs left the room and never found the door unlocked again. When she realized that her story was not believed, she held her peace concerning the whole affair.

But Mrs. Griggs had told no more than the simple truth. Jasper Dale, under all that shyness, possessed a nature full of delicate romance, which denied expression in the common ways of life. Left alone by his mother's death, just when the boy's nature was deepening to manhood, he turned to an imaginary life. He believed the real world could never give him love, and so he created in his imagination the image of the woman he would have liked to love. Soon the loving and kind woman of his dreams became almost as real to him as his own personality. He cherished her and gave her the name he liked best—Alice.

In his imagination, he walked and talked with her, spoke words of love to her, and heard words of love in return. When he came home from work at the close of the day, he imagined that she met him at the threshold in the twilight.

One day when he was in Charlottetown on business, he became interested in a picture he saw in the window of a store. It was strangely like the woman of his dreams. Though he felt awkward and embarrassed, he went in and bought it. Once at home, he wasn't sure where to put it. It seemed out of place among his mother's older pictures. Then he had an inspiration. He would hang the picture in a room that would belong exclusively to the woman of his dreams. He would decorate the room the way he thought she would like it.

Jasper Dale spent all summer carrying out his plan, working slowly and secretly so no one would suspect. One by one, he purchased the furnishings and brought them home after dark, carefully arranging them in the room. He bought the books he imagined she would like best and wrote her name in them. He got the feminine knickknacks— the basket and thimble—and the pale blue dress with the satin slippers. He had always fancied her as dressed in blue.

One spring Alice Reade came to teach music in Carlisle. Her students worshiped her, but the grown people thought her to be distant and reserved. They had been used to beautiful, fun girls who joined eagerly in the social life of the town. Alice Reade held herself aloof, as one who doesn't find social life important. She wasn't shy but was as sensitive as a flower. After a time the people of Carlisle were content to let her live her own life and no longer resented the fact that she was different.

She boarded with the Armstrongs, who lived beyond Golden Milestone around the Hill of Pines. Until the snow disappeared in the spring, she went out to the main road and walked along Armstrong Lane. But when spring came, she took a shorter way down the Pine Hill and across the brook, past Jasper Dale's garden and out through his lane. One day when she went by, Jasper was working in his garden.

He was on his knees in a corner planting some bulbs that would someday be lovely flowers. It was a still spring morning, and the world was green with young leaves. A little wind blew down from the pines and stirred the budding delights of the garden. The wind opened the eyes of blue violets. The sky was high and cloudless, and birds were singing down the brook valley. Jolly robins were whistling joyfully in the pines. Jasper Dale's heart was overflowing with the realization of all the loveliness around him. There was a feeling in his soul like a sacred prayer. At that very moment he looked up and saw Alice Reade.

She was standing outside the garden fence in the shadow of a great pine tree. She was not looking at him, for she didn't even know he was nearby. But she was looking at the beautiful flowering plum trees in the far corner.

For a moment Jasper believed his dream had come true. She was not exactly like his imaginary Alice—at least not in her face. But in grace and coloring, she was exactly what he had imagined. His whole soul leaped up to meet and welcome her.

Then her eyes fell upon him, and the spell was broken. Jasper continued kneeling silently, pretending to work in his garden. The shy man, a strange, almost pitiful creature, was completely lost in love.

As for Miss Reade, a little smile flickered across the delicate corners of her mouth as she turned and walked quickly away down the lane. Jasper looked after her with a painful sense of loss and loveliness. It had been agony to feel her eyes upon him, but he realized now that there had been a strange sweetness in it too. It was a greater pain to watch her moving away from him.

He guessed that she was the new music teacher. He had never known her name, but he was sure it must be Alice. She had been dressed in blue too—a pale dainty blue, just as he had always imagined her.

Now he could only think of the Alice who had stood under the tree, not the shadowy spirit of the west gable room. He didn't realize what all this meant, but he did know that he had a curious sense of loss.

That afternoon Jasper saw her on her way home. She didn't pause by the garden but walked swiftly past. Every day that week he watched her as she passed by to go home, but he was careful not to let her see him watching.

The next day he failed for the first time to put flowers in the west gable room. Instead he cut a loose handful of daffodils. Looking about to be sure that no one was watching, he laid the beautiful flowers on the footpath where Alice would pass. From his safe retreat, he saw her stoop to get the flowers. From that day on he put flowers in the same place every day.

When Alice Reade saw the flowers, she knew at once who had put them there and that they were for her. She lifted them tenderly with much surprise and pleasure. She thought his face and dark blue eyes were handsome.

When she heard the story of the locked room, she believed it might be true. It made the shy man seem more interesting and romantic. She thought that she would like to solve the mystery and unlock the key to his character.

Each day when she found flowers under the pine tree, she felt a growing desire to see Jasper and thank him. She was totally unaware that he watched her every day from the screen of shrubbery in his garden. It was some time before she got the opportunity to speak to him. One evening she passed when he was not expecting her, and she saw him leaning against his garden fence with a book in his hand. She stopped under the pine.

104

"Mr. Dale," she said softly, "I want to thank you for your flowers."

Jasper was so startled that he wished he might sink into the ground. He was so embarrassed that it made her smile a little. He did not speak, so she spoke again quietly.

"It has been so good of you to give me the lovely flowers. They have given me great pleasure—I wish you could know how much."

"It was nothing—nothing," stammered Jasper. His book had fallen on the ground at her feet, and she picked it up and held it out to him.

"So you like the author, Rufkin," she said. "I do too, but I haven't read this one."

"If you—would care—to read it—you may have it," Jasper managed to say. So she carried the book away with her.

Jasper did not hide the next time she passed. When she brought the book back, they talked a little bit about it over the fence. He loaned others to her and borrowed some from her in return. Soon they fell into the habit of discussing the books. Jasper didn't find it hard to talk to her now, and Alice seemed to think what he had to say was worthwhile. His words stayed in her memory and made music in her soul. She always found his flowers under the pine tree and always wore some of them. She wasn't sure if he noticed this or not.

One evening Jasper walked shyly with her from his gate up the Pine Hill. After that he always walked that far with her. She would have missed him very much if he had failed to do so, yet it didn't occur to her that she was learning to love him. She would have laughed with scorn at the idea. She liked him very much and thought his nature was kind in its simplicity and purity. In spite of his shyness, she felt delightfully at home with him, more than with any other person.

On a lovely August day, she saw him sitting on a rustic bench on the farther side with his back turned toward her, reading a book. He was partially hidden by a large group of lilacs. He didn't hear her footsteps, and she was close behind him when she heard his voice. She realized that he was talking to himself in a low dreamy tone. As the meaning of his words dawned on her, she started to turn red with embarrassment. She couldn't move or speak and stood as one in a dream, listening to the shy man's conversation with himself.

"I love you so much, Alice," Jasper Dale was saying. He was unafraid with no shyness in his manner. "I wonder what you would say if you knew? You would laugh at me, sweet as you are. You would laugh in mockery. That's why I can never tell you. I can only dream of telling you. In my dream you are standing here by me, dear. I see you very plainly, my sweet lady, so tall and gracious with your dark hair and sweet eyes. I can dream that you love me in return. Everything is possible in dreams, you know. My dreams are all I have, so I go far in them, even to dreaming that you are my wife.

"I dream of how I shall fix up my dull old house for you. One room will need nothing more—it is your room and has been ready for you a long time. It's been ready since before that day I saw you under the pine trees. Your books and your chair and your picture are there. Only the picture is not half lovely enough.

"I would see you sitting in your own chair, and then all my dreams would find rich fulfillment in that one moment. We would have a beautiful life together. It's sweet to make-believe about it—you will sing to me in the twilight, and we will gather early flowers together in the spring days. When I come home from work tired, you will put your arms around me and lay your head on my shoulder. Alice, my Alice—all mine in my dreams—never to be mine in real life—how I love you!"

The real Alice, who was standing behind him, could bear no more. She gave a choking little cry that gave away her presence. Jasper Dale sprang up and looked at her. He saw her standing there among the shadows of August, pale with feeling, wide-eyed and trembling. For a moment shyness overcame him. Then every trace of the shyness was banished by a sudden, strange, fierce anger that swept over him. He felt outraged and mortified to death. He felt that he had been cheated out of something precious, as if damage had been done to his most holy emotions. White with anger, he looked at her and spoke. His lips were pale as if fiery words had scorched them.

"How dare you! You have spied on me! You have crept in and listened! How could you? Do you know what you have done, girl? You have destroyed all that made life worthwhile for me. My dream is dead. It can't live once betrayed, and it was all I had. Go on and laugh at me—mock me. I know that I'm ridiculous!"

"Jasper!" cried Alice, finding her voice. His anger hurt her with a pain she couldn't endure. It was unbearable that Jasper should be angry with her. In that moment she realized that she loved him. She realized that the words he had spoken when he didn't know she was there were the sweetest she had ever heard.

"Don't say such dreadful things to me," she stammered. "I didn't mean to listen. I couldn't help it. I shall never laugh at you! Oh, Jasper, I am glad that you love me! And I am glad that I chanced to overhear you since you would never have had the courage to tell me otherwise. Glad—glad. Do you understand, Jasper?"

Jasper looked at her with the eyes of one looking through pain and saw rapture beyond. "Is it possible?" he said wonderingly. "Alice, I am so much older than you, and they call me the Awkward Man. They say I am unlike other people."

"You *are* unlike other people," she said softly. "That is why I love you. I know now that I must have loved you ever since I first saw you."

"I loved you long before I knew you," said Jasper. He came close to her and drew her into his arms as all his shyness and awkwardness disappeared. In the old garden, he kissed her and Alice became his own love.

It was at that time that he went into the house and got his mother's wedding ring, a beautiful blue sapphire encircled with diamonds. When he placed it on Alice Reade's finger, it was as though he glorified her with his love. Alice was the happiest girl alive. It did not matter what anyone in Carlisle thought. Jasper Dale had found his Beautiful Alice.

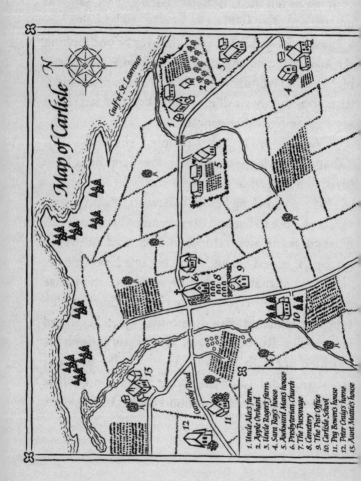

Map of Carlisle

N

Gulf of St. Lawrence

Carmody Road

1. Uncle Alec's farm
2. Apple Orchard
3. Uncle Roger's farm
4. Sam Ray's house
5. Awkward Man's house
6. Presbyterian Church
7. The Parsonage
8. Cemetery
9. The Post Office
10. Carlisle School
11. Peg Bowen's house
12. Peter Craig's home
13. Aunt Mattie's house

Lucy Maud Montgomery
1874-1942

Anne of Green Gables was the very first book that Lucy Maud Montgomery published. In all, she wrote twenty-five books.

Lucy Maud Montgomery was born on Prince Edward Island. Her family called her Maud. Before she was two years old, her mother died and she was sent to live with her mother's parents on their farm on the Island. Her grandparents were elderly and very strict. Maud lived with them for a long time.

When she was seven, her father remarried. He moved far out west to Saskatchewan, Canada, with his new wife. At age seventeen, she went to live with them, but she did not get along with her stepmother. So she returned to her grandparents.

She attended college and studied to become a teacher—just like Anne in the Avonlea series. When her grandfather died, Maud went home to be with her grandmother. Living there in the quiet of Prince Edward Island, she had plenty of time to write. It was during this time that she wrote her first book, *Anne of Green Gables*. When the book was finally accepted, it was published soon after. It was an immediate hit, and Maud began to get thousands of letters asking for more stories about Anne. She wrote *Anne of Avonlea, Chronicles of Avonlea, Anne of the Island, Anne of Windy Poplars, Anne's House of Dreams, Rainbow Valley, Anne of Ingleside,* and *Rilla of Ingleside.* She also wrote *The Story Girl* and *The Golden Road.*

When Maud was thirty-seven years old, Ewan Macdonald, the minister of the local Presbyterian Church in Canvendish, proposed marriage to her. Maud accepted and they were married. Later on they moved to Ontario where two sons, Chester and Stewart, were born to the couple.

Maud never went back to Prince Edward Island to live again. But when she died in 1942, she was buried on the Island, near the house known as Green Gables.

zonder**kidz**.

We want to hear from you. Please send your comments
about this book to us in care of zreview@zondervan.com. Thank you.

Grand Rapids, MI 49530
www.zonderkidz.com